14.95

DATE DUE

JUL 2 0 2004	NOV 7 2005
AUG 0 3 2004	NOV 1 7 2005
AUG 1 3 2004	MAR 1 7 2006
JAN 1 1 2005	JUN 3 0 2006
FEB 0 1 2005	
JUL 0 5 2005	
JUL 0 5 2005	
JUL 2 0 2005	
AUG 0 3 2005	

ST. JOHN THE BAPTIST PARISH LIBRARY
1334 WEST AIRLINE HIGHWAY
LaPLACE, LOUISIANA 70068

D1445381

For Isabel and Carl

—P. M.

To my parents, Irene and Jimmy

—C. M.

 Bill Martin Jr, Ph.D., has devoted his life to the education of young children. *Bill Martin Books* reflect his philosophy: that children's imaginations are opened up through the play of language, the imagery of illustration, and the permanent joy of reading books.

Henry Holt and Company, Inc.
Publishers since 1866
115 West 18th Street
New York, New York 10011

Henry Holt is a registered
trademark of Henry Holt and Company, Inc.
Text copyright © 1994 by Peter Mandel
Illustrations copyright © 1994 by Clare Mackie
All rights reserved.
Published in Canada by Fitzhenry & Whiteside Ltd.,
195 Allstate Parkway, Markham, Ontario L3R 4T8.

Library of Congress Cataloging-in-Publication Data
Mandel, Peter.
Red cat, white cat / by Peter Mandel ; illustrations by Clare Mackie.
"A Bill Martin book."
1. English language—Synonyms and antonyms—Juvenile literature.
[1. English language—Synonyms and antonyms. 2. Cats.]
I. Mackie, Clare, ill. II. Title. PE1591.M34 1994 428.1—dc20 93-47048

ISBN 0-8050-2929-X

First Edition—1994
Printed in the United States of America
on acid-free paper. ∞
1   3   5   7   9   10   8   6   4   2

Red Cat White Cat

Peter Mandel

Illustrations by Clare Mackie

· *A Bill Martin Book* ·

Henry Holt and Company ❋ New York

Red Cat,

White Cat...

Day Cat,

Night Cat.

Short Cat,

Tall Cat...

Spring Cat,

Fall Cat.

In Cat,

Out Cat...

Thin Cat,

Stout Cat.

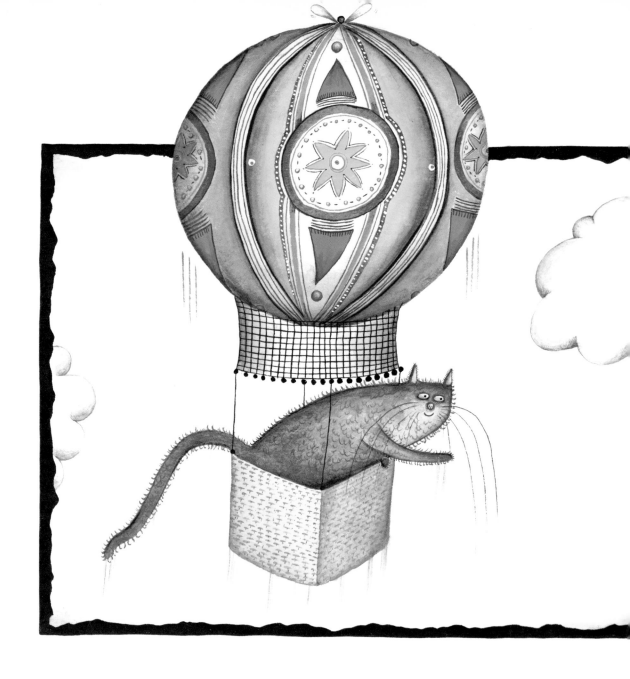

Up Cat,

Down Cat...

Farm Cat,

Town · Cat.

Hot Cat,

Cold Cat...

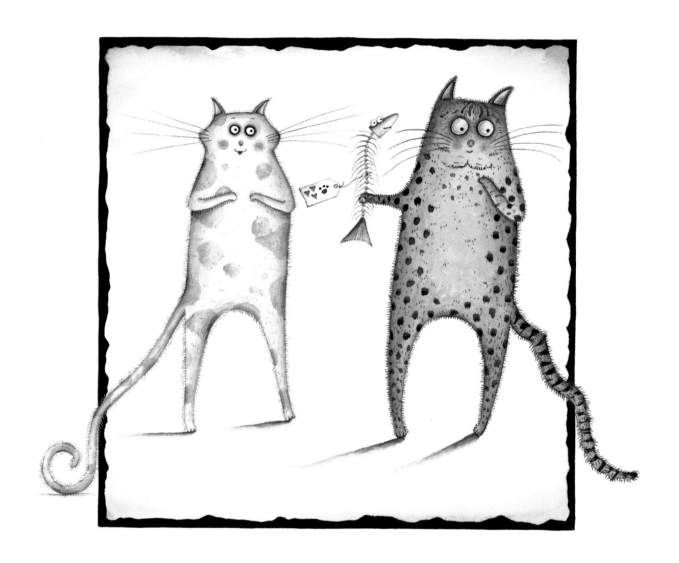

Shy Cat,

Bold Cat.

Wet Cat,

Dry Cat...

Your Cat,

My Cat.

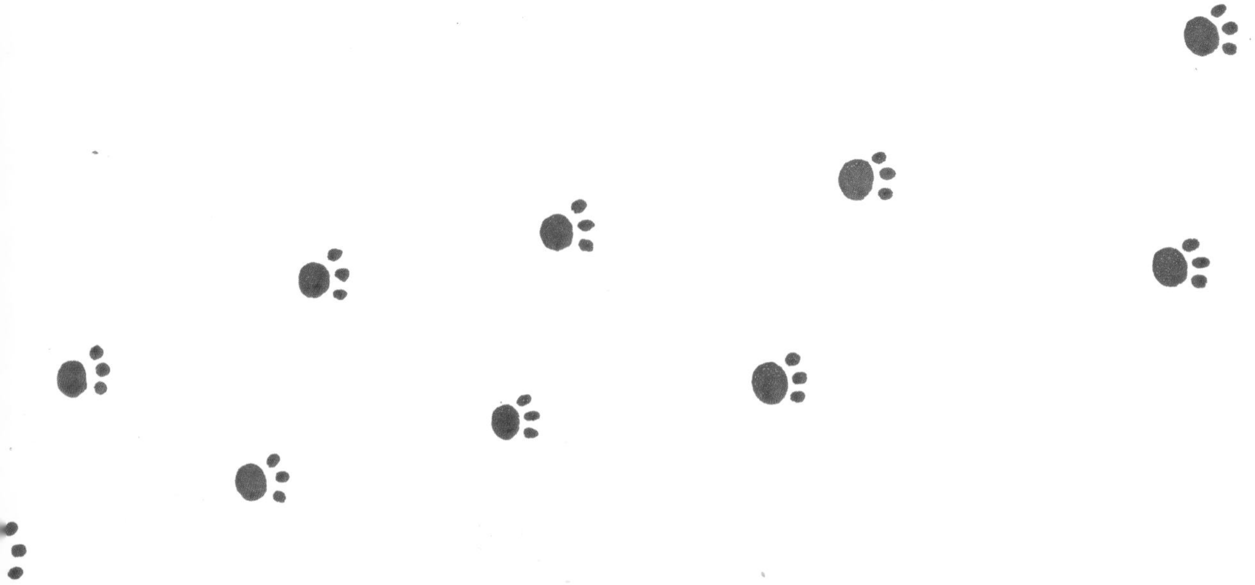